Baboon Troops

Written by Jo Windsor

CONTENTS

BABOON TROOPS

Baboons are large monkeys. They live together in a group called a troop. Some troops are small. Some troops are big.

Each baboon has a place in the troop. There are animals at the top and animals at the bottom. Every baboon must keep to his or her place in the troop order. A troop works well when all the animals know and obey the rules.

A PLACE FOR

At the top of the troop order is a big male baboon. He is the leader. He takes the best sleeping places in a tree,

4

ALL

and the best food and water. He will defend
his place at the top of the troop. He will snarl,
showing his long sharp teeth, and sometimes
he will bite.

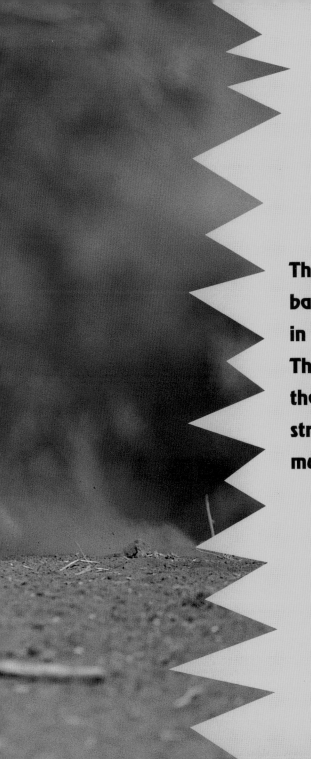

The other strong male baboons are the next in the troop order. They know that the leader is the strongest and they must obey the rules.

The females with babies are next in the troop order. The baby baboons will stay with their mothers for up to five years.

(The older females that have
no babies are the last
in the troop order.)

The young baboons that have just left their mothers are the next in the troop order. They play in small groups. They learn how to chase and fight.

Leader

Strong Male Baboons

Females with Babies

Young Baboons

Older Females

LIVING IN A

At the beginning of the day, the troop moves off to look for food. They like to eat fruit, nuts, leaves, roots and small animals. When the troop moves from place to place, they go in a special pattern that helps to protect the troop from danger.

Did you know . . . ?

When baboons travel, the strong young males go at the front of the troop. They give the alarm if an enemy comes near. Other males travel in the middle of the troop and at the back of the troop. They protect the mothers and babies.

TROOP

Between meals, baboons groom one another. They use their long fingers to remove dirt and pests from each other's coats. This helps to keep the baboons clean.

At night, the troop sleeps in a clump of trees. Each baboon knows the rules to obey about who sleeps where.

Index

Reports

REPORTS record information.

HOW TO WRITE A REPORT

Step One
- ☐ **Choose a topic.**
- ☐ **Make a list of the things you know about the topic.**

Topic:
    Baboon Troops
<u>What I know:</u>
- Baboons are large monkeys.
- Baboons live in a troop.
- Baboons h

- ☐ **Write down the things you need to find out.**

<u>What I would like to find out:</u>
- Things about the leader of the troop.
- Things about other baboons.
- What baboons like to eat.

Step Two

☐ **Find out about the things you need to know. You can:**

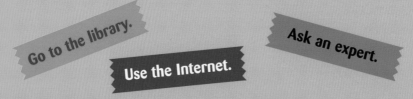

Go to the library.

Use the Internet.

Ask an expert.

☐ **Make notes!**

Step Three

☐ **Organize the information. Make some headings.**

Members of the troop:	What baboon troops eat:	Where a troop sleeps:
• Leaders • Strong males • Females with babies	• Fruit • Leaves • Roots • Nuts	• In trees—the leader takes the best sleeping place.

Step Four

☐ **Use your notes to write your report!**

☐ **You can use:**
diagrams, labels, illustrations, photographs, charts, tables, and graphs.

Guide Notes

Title: Baboon Troops
Stage: Fluency (1)

Text Form: Informational Report
Approach: Guided Reading
Processes: Thinking Critically, Exploring Language, Processing Information
Written and Visual Focus: Photographs, Index, Contents Page, Schematic Diagram

---

THINKING CRITICALLY
(sample questions)
- What do you think this story is going to tell us?
- Focus the children's attention on the contents. Ask: "What things are you going to find out about in this book?"
- Look at the index. Ask: "What are the things you want to find out about baboons? What page would you turn to in the book?"
- Why do you think baboons live together in a troop?
- Why do you think a baboon troop has rules?

EXPLORING LANGUAGE

Terminology
Photograph credits, imprint information, ISBN number, index, contents

Vocabulary
Clarify: troop, obey, defend, snarl, groom, protect
Nouns: monkey, troop, member, female
Verbs: bite, play, eat
Singular/plural: baby/babies, baboon/baboons, group/groups

Print Conventions
Apostrophe – possessive (each other's coats)

Phonological Patterns
Focus on long and short vowel sound **a** (baboon, sharp, last, baby, **a**ttack)
Look at suffix **ing** (sleep**ing**), **est** (strong**est**)